Bear and the Mysterious Downstairs

Written by Olivia Oo
Illustrated by Eugenia Pro

Edited by Bingying Luo
and Germaine Goh

Once upon a time, Bear lived with her friend Panda on a big bed.

One day, Bear decided it was time for her to leave the comfort of the bed. She longed for adventures in the big outside world.

Perhaps she could also make some new friends, she thought.

So, Bear made her way to the door
and bid farewell to Panda.

"I'm going to miss you so much!"
Panda said to her friend, blinking back
tears and waving as hard as she could.

The outside world was big and scary. Even the initial trip down the stairs was hard. However, Bear persevered because she very much wanted to see the world.

There were often obstacles in Bear's path. There were people who seemed friendly at first, but ended up pulling on her ears for no apparent reason.

Bear was brave. She continued on her adventure and did not flinch one bit.

Soon, Bear came to a big, scary door.
She was afraid because she did not know
what she would find behind it.

It could be a huge, hairy monster.
Or an evil witch. Or a smelly skeleton
doing maths homework.

Or maybe, just maybe, she would
find a friend there.

Bear crept into the room, and
peered out from behind the bed.
She spotted a girl in a yellow shirt.

Yes, Bear decided, she looks nice.
I want to be her friend.

Bear climbed up the side of the bed. After much effort, she managed to get onto the table. The girl extended her hand towards Bear, like she wanted to shake hands. Bear felt all warm and fuzzy inside.

To Bear's horror, the girl bonked her on the head! Tears rolled down Bear's cheeks. I guess the girl doesn't want to be friends after all, she thought to herself sadly.

Through her tears, Bear saw the girl in yellow raise her fist of fury again. She was getting ready to bonk Bear on the head once more!

Suddenly, to everyone's surprise, there was a yell from the door. Panda had appeared!

"Stop!" shouted Panda with great concern. "Bear! Are you okay?"

"And what do YOU want?" asked the girl in yellow.

Panda was not intimidated. "I'm here to rescue my friend," she replied.

With that, Panda gave a brave battle cry and leapt onto the girl's leg! The girl yelped in shock.

Then, Bear joined in and jumped onto the girl's face!
There was nothing she could do about it.

Before long, the two friends had overpowered the girl in yellow. She sank to the ground, tired and defeated.

Just then, a girl in black burst in.

"What is happening over here?" she exclaimed. She quickly pulled Bear and Panda away from the girl in yellow.

The two friends tried to explain
how Bear had tried so hard to become
friends with the girl in yellow,
only to be bonked on the head.

"We make new friends and win people
over with kindness and sincerity,"
the girl in black said sternly to Bear and
Panda, "Not by fighting with them."

The girl in yellow looked very surprised.
"Did you say 'make friends'? Is that
what Bear wanted to do?" she asked.

Everyone nodded.

"I'm so sorry! I had no idea!
Can we start over?" she said.

Over strawberry smoothies, everyone introduced themselves to each other. They realised they had a lot in common, like a love for bagels and singing in the shower.

The girl in yellow said, "I've never met a bear before. I never imagined that someone so different from me would want to be my friend."

Eventually, it was time for Bear and Panda to go home. The girl in black said that she would take them home and make sure they were safe.

The girl in yellow promised that they could visit anytime.

Everyone had learnt a lot that day.

The girl in yellow realised that anyone could become a friend, even those who seem so different.

And Bear and Panda now knew that even if someone seemed like they didn't want to be friends, they should still be treated with kindness and sincerity.

Best of all, everyone had made a new friend that day.

For my husband ~ Thank you for your
love and support.

For my children, Lexie and Amber ~ May the
magic of reading stay with you always.

~ Olivia

Text copyright by Olivia Oo
Illustrations copyright by Eugenia Pro

Edited by Bingying Luo and Germaine Goh

ISBN 979 85 60538 24 8

About the author:

Olivia lives in Singapore. She has two daughters and a small dog named Snuggles. This book was first born in Berkeley, CA, when she coerced her college housemates and good friends Bingying and Germaine to, among other crazy activities, take a series of photos featuring them attacking a stuffed bear while she provided appropriate captions. Almost 20 years later, the old photos and texts surfaced, and with Eugenia's help, the bear's story is born again.

About the illustrator:

Eugenia lives in Amsterdam with her partner and little son. After years of work as a digital designer, she was drawn naturally toward the fascinating world of illustration. She's spent most of her life living in Ukraine before settling in Amsterdam, but travelling remains a constant in her life. Permanently in touch with a range of different cultures, she has developed a great sense of adaptation. That's why she finds this collaboration with Olivia so exciting!

Made in the USA
Middletown, DE
06 June 2023

32146224R00018